S0-BRR-541

3 0000 380 032 628

WITHDRAWN

for Sophia, Lionni and Ronni

Rocky Pond Books
An imprint of Penguin Random House LLC, New York

First published in the United States of America by Rocky Pond Books, an imprint of Penguin Random House LLC, 2023

Copyright © 2023 by Daniel Salmieri

Penguin supports copyright. Copyright fuels creativity, encourages diverse voices, promotes free speech, and creates a vibrant culture. Thank you for buying an authorized edition of this book and for complying with copyright laws by not reproducing, scanning, or distributing any part of it in any form without permission. You are supporting writers and allowing Penguin to continue to publish books for every reader.

Rocky Pond Books & colophon are trademarks of Penguin Random House LLC. The Penguin colophon is a registered trademark of Penguin Books Limited.

Visit us online at penguinrandomhouse.com.
Library of Congress Cataloging-in-Publication Data is available.

Manufactured in China • ISBN 9780593461976 • 10 9 8 7 6 5 4 3 2 1
TOPL

Design by Lily Malcom • Text set in GT Walsheim

The art for this book was created with colored pencil on paper.

BEFORE, NOW

by Daniel Salmieri

Rocky Pond Books

INDIANA STATE UNIVERSITY LIBRARY

In the dark sky floats a bright planet

Where wet waves crash on a dry stretch of beach
And there are smooth stones in the rough sand

Dew shines on the dull bark of a tree
Outside a little home on a big street

In the home there's a small person in a big chair
And squishy oatmeal in a hard bowl

There are fluffy birds in a prickly nest

And pointy teeth in a round snout

A cold jacket on a warm face

And vivid dreams of vast spaces
inside a small head

Colorful sneakers skip down a gray sidewalk

And light balloons float above
a heavy picnic table

There are near faces against the distant stars

And a loud concert in a quiet field

Thick books made up of thin sheets of paper

And invisible movement seen
through the lens of a microscope

A speeding train in a still station

And bright lightning in a dark cloud

There is squishy oatmeal in a hard bowl

Wet waves into a dry sandcastle

And an old photo in a new frame
Shows a picture of a small person in a big chair